STERLING CHILDREN'S BOOKS
New York

An Imprint of Sterling Publishing
387 Park Avenue South
New York, NY 10016

ISBN 978-1-4027-8436-1

Distributed in Canada by Sterling Publishing
c/o Canadian Manda Group, 165 Dufferin Street
Toronto, Ontario, Canada M6K 3H6
Distributed in the United Kingdom by GMC Distribution Services
Castle Place, 166 High Street, Lewes, East Sussex, England BN7 1XU
Distributed in Australia by Capricorn Link (Australia) Pty. Ltd.
P.O. Box 704, Windsor, NSW 2756, Australia

For information about custom editions, special sales, and premium and corporate
purchases, please contact Sterling Special Sales at 800-805-5489
or specialsales@sterlingpublishing.com.

Printed in China
Lot #:
2 4 6 8 10 9 7 5 3 1
07/13

www.sterlingpublishing.com/kids

SILVER PENNY STORIES

The Princess and the Pea

Told by Diane Namm
Illustrated by Linda Olafsdottir

Once upon a time there was a handsome young prince.

"It is time for me to marry," he announced to his parents. "And I wish to marry a real princess."

"Then you must search for her, my son," the queen said.

"How will I know if she's a real princess?" asked the prince.

"You will just know," promised the queen.

The prince mounted his horse.

"I'll find a real princess, no matter how long it takes or how far I must ride," he said.

The prince rode until he came to the North Kingdom.

The loveliest girl in the north shouted, "I WOULD LIKE TO BE YOUR PRINCESS!"

The very hills of the valley echoed.

This girl cannot be my princess.
Her loud voice really annoys me,
the prince thought.

He mounted his horse and rode until
he came to the South Kingdom.

"I'd like to be your princess,"
said the loveliest girl in the south.
"Please stay for dinner."

As they ate, the prince waited
for a sign.

The lovely young girl brought her glass of water to her lips.

Slurp, slurp, slurrrrp was all the prince heard.

"I must be going now," the prince said.

The prince rode until he came
to the East Kingdom.

He was greeted by the loveliest
girl in the east—*and* her mother.

"My daughter would like to be
your princess," said the mother.

"Let's walk in the garden," suggested the prince.

So the prince, the girl, and the mother strolled among the flowers.

The birds chirped, the bees hummed, and the girl's mother chattered.

"Do *you* ever speak?" the prince asked the lovely girl.

"Young girls should be seen and not heard," her mother said.

"Then I'll be on my way," the prince said.

The prince rode far and wide until he came to the West Kingdom.

"You WILL make me your princess! I demand it!" ordered the loveliest girl in the west.

The prince didn't even bother to get off his horse.

The prince returned to his kingdom feeling very sad.

"I'll never find a real princess," he told the king and queen.

He was just about to go to bed when . . .

. . . a storm broke out.

Thunder clapped. Lightning struck.
Suddenly, they heard a knock on the
castle door. In the doorway stood the
most beautiful young woman
the prince had ever seen.

"My dear, you're soaking wet," said the queen. "You must stay the night."

"Mother," the prince whispered. "Is she . . ?"

"We shall find out," the queen said.

"Tell us your story, my dear," the queen said, giving her a cup of tea. "Then I'll prepare your room."

"Thank you," the young woman said in a lovely, musical voice. She sipped her tea delicately and explained how she had lost her kingdom to an evil wizard.

The prince was sure this sweet and charming guest was a real princess.

"We shall know by tomorrow," his mother whispered to him.

Then she showed the young woman to a bedroom.

In the young woman's room was a large bed. On that bed were twenty feather pillows and twenty feather beds upon twenty royal mattresses.

Beneath it all, the queen had slipped a tiny pea.

The young woman tossed and turned all night. No matter how hard she tried, she couldn't fall asleep.

The next morning, the queen asked, "How did you sleep, my dear?"

"I'm sorry, but I did not sleep at all," she said gently. "I believe there may have been a stone underneath my mattress. But thank you so much for your kindness. I am very lucky to have escaped that terrible storm."

The prince and queen knew that only a real princess could have felt the pea.

The prince was overjoyed. He loved her. He fell in love with her the moment they met.

Without waiting any longer, he asked, "Will you be my bride?"

"I will," she replied with a kiss.

They married at once and lived happily ever after.